Tab

The Last Witch-Queen of Raven

Prologue	5
Part One: Raven, City of Salt and Silver	7
Part Two: Under Manticore and Moon	9
Part Three: From Child to Woman	13
Part Four: Monsters of Shadow and Sand	15
Part Five: The Witch-Queen's Rule	21
Part Six: Fifty Days	23
Part Seven: One Deadly Dance	31
Part Eight: Whispers of Hope	35
Part Nine: The Head of a Monster	39
Part Ten: Long Knives, Longer Shadows	43
Epilogue: Another story, perhaps?	47

Ky's Korner Productions books by Triston Pethybridge

The Amalia Chronicles
The Last Witch-Queen of Raven (an origin story)

Ky's Korner Productions books by Kyleen McHenry

Gods and Titans
#1: Blackbirds: Life of a Thief—available August 2023

The Last Witch-Queen of Raven
The Amalia Chronicles

Written by Triston Pethybridge
Original Concept by Kyleen McHenry

Copyright © 2023 Ky's Korner Productions, LLC

All rights reserved. No part of this publication may be reproduced, distributed, or transmitted in any form or by any means, including photocopying, recording, or other electronic or mechanical methods, without the prior written permission of the publisher, except in the case of brief quotations embodied in critical reviews and certain other noncommercial uses permitted by copyright law. For permission requests, write to the publisher, addressed "Attention: Permissions Coordinator," at the address below.

Any references to historical events, real people, or real places are used fictitiously. Names, characters, and places are products of the author's imagination.

Front cover image by Kyleen McHenry

Published in 2023 by Ky's Korner Productions, LLC
    PO Box 874
    Berwick, PA 18603
    United States
    www.kyskornerproductions.com

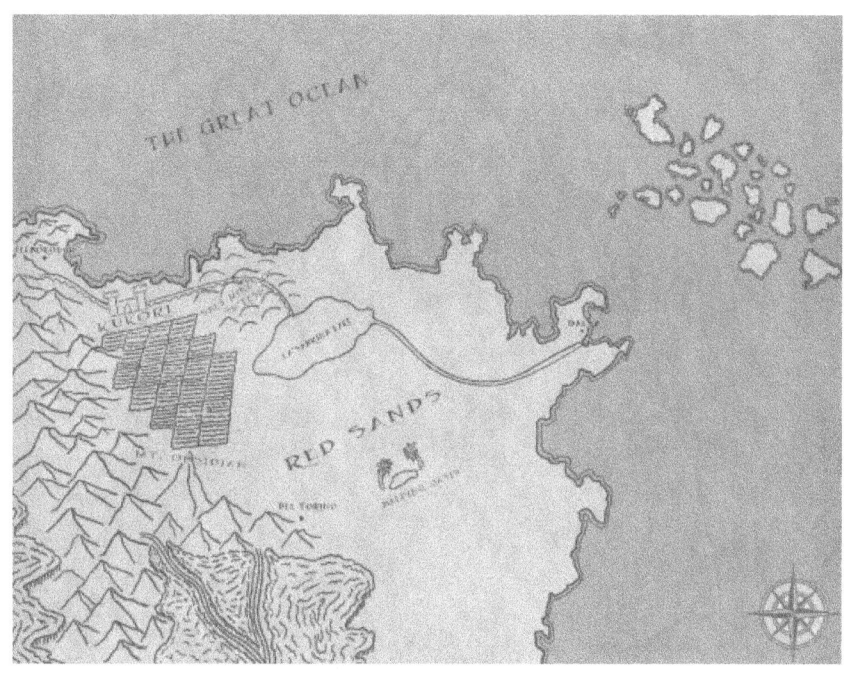

Prologue

Blood. Blood trickled down the streets, between the cracks of the paving stones It flowed like dirty water and spread like ink over the icy ground.

The blood slowly streamed from me, mingling with earth and stone. The blood mingled with that of fallen foes and friends alike. The nearby flames caused shadows to dance and leap from wall, to street, and back again.

Distant shouts and screams pierced the night, pained, miserable whimpers from the dying around me.

The sounds of several warriors and the hoof claps of a single horse started winding their way closer and closer, but unsure in that moment of danger, I remained still and quiet.

Soldiers dressed in the armor and shadow black cloaks of the royal guard along with a woman on horseback eventually came into view.

Armor clanked over galloping hooves, and the shouting of orders in the distance. The sounds got closer and closer. I thought about running, hiding, and preserving myself but thought better of it.

The blackened bronze of their armor identified them as the royal guard. Their helms and neck guards blinded their peripheral vision, allowing onlookers to stare as they passed by. The figure on the horse was, at first, a mystery to me.

Only when the light from errant flame danced did I begin to recognize the face of my queen.

Part One: Raven, City of Salt and Silver

Waking in the morning of the mid spring always imparts a sense of curiosity. Will it be raining? Will the clouds form a blanket across the sky? Will the brilliant light of the sun cascade across the streets, making things comfortably warm and inviting? Perhaps today the city will have all three of these things come to pass three times throughout the day.

I am Myron Taxidis, and if you have been so bold, so daring, as to pick up this tome, then my beloved reader, prepare for adventure.

This dark tale is the creation of long forgotten shadows in a time before our peace and tranquility. The events are as true to their time in these records, I can assure you.

I have had to do my best in cross-examination of the conflicting records and had to take a limited creative license to the events merely alluded to.

The record of every small interaction between subjects, soldiers, oligarchs, and foreign dignitaries is lost to the ever-shifting flow of time.

This story is an important reminder to those who would rule now, as well as those who would rule in the future. It is a reminder of how quickly a ruler can change.

Of course, to understand the city in the past, you will have to understand the present course the city is on. The city of Raven sits along the coast of the great ocean, far afield from its neighboring city-states.

The city is situated next to a natural harbor that is home to a great variety and quantity of sea creatures that are harvested by the population. To the east, within partial days walk of the east gate are the salt fields that have been mined for many generations.

These fields provide an ample supply of salt which has been instrumental in bringing us into contact with our mountain neighbors.

Our neighbors in the mountains constructed an aqueduct from the lake to help supply the growing mining camp in exchange for the salt and some additional mining labor.

Feeding a city of thousands would not be possible without such cooperation. The nearby farms provide grain and other crops while herders living in the foothills of the mountains bring their flocks to market to provide a supply of meat to the masses.

Some of the places we call home are also made of the very salt that we mine. Children run up and down the paved streets between shops and houses, and merchants ply their trade in the open-air market of the city.

The city itself is not without its distractions and its places for the idle or halls for criminal activity. No, like any city, it has smudges on its face. The buildings made of cheap brick are small cells for people to call home.

They are a breeding ground for many of the society's maladies, and the adverse conditions do leave the poorest of them with little hope or recourse. There are lords and beggars, just like any other place.

Finally, we must look to the families that are of the highest order. Twenty-four such families date their lineages back to a time just after the fall of the last despot of this city.

Each has granted me some insight of their lineage and records that were collected in the aftermath of the downfall.

Other records come from the academic hall, a fanciful library with nearly five hundred scrolls and illuminated texts within its walls.

The bardic institution was less forthcoming. The instructors seem to think it an age of baseless art and song meant only to make beautiful a despot whose soul was vile to its black core.

Other tales kept as base records of services purchased by those of the lower strata, kept as some reminder of dark deeds rendered for gold.

All of this combines to illustrate how one wielding power can accomplish greatness, both vile and wonderous.

Part Two: Under Manticore and Moon

From the records of the church of Zuzara, Protector of Motherhood, Keeper of the Hearth, Lady of Fidelity:

"On moon's day, in the time of year that is our second harvest, in the fifth year of the reign of King Arkouda in the city of Kukori, in the hour of twilight, the Geropalides family brought a baby girl into this world.

The child, Ariadne, was born under the watchful gaze of Priestess Irini and her two attendants, Cyra and Anzoy.

The Manticore constellation was seen hanging in the northern sky with a sliver of the moon passing near its open mouth.

Ariadne is so written as to be the eldest of the union of Geropalides and Archiplousios. This union of the members of these houses carries the blessing of Zuzara."

This is a very common record keeping for those within the clergy of Zuzara. The events of the birth are further recorded.

"The child was born quickly as from the moment of the passing of water, to the moment of birth, all took place within the space of twilight."

"Upon inspection of the child"—the priestess most likely dictated this for writing—"I came across no such markings or malforms. The child is healthy from everything I can see and feel.

Her eyes seem to be either blue or green in the candlelight, and her few hairs are blonde, similar to her mothers." These humble records of the birth of this little girl seem to be the best candidate for the truth.

This record has a statement in contradiction to this document, as amended by Anzoy, "This amendment, to the record of the birth of Ariadne, is to correct an oversight in the inspection of the child.

"While not clearly visible in the light of the candles, the daylight did show a mild discoloration of the skin over the heart of the child. These pale spots do not seem to lack a flow of vitality but do lack the rosy pigment of the rest of the body."

These are the final clues of my investigation to the actual identity of the despot.

For the time and events to occur as such, these are my findings within the record of known births, within the city that would make the child old enough to become the ruler in question.

Conventional thought is a person would have to come from the ruling classes to have the connections and wealth to have political relevance and be able to wield magick, and specifically the powers of a nevrokarna.

These pale spots are an indication of the potential for nevrokarna. The attached record of astrology is also of note. The records of the reading say, "Those born under the Manticore are proud and regal regardless to station born.

They are powerful individuals capable of being strong leaders with a natural gift for words. This strength of voice and posture will both intimidate and inspire, and if matched in an alluring visage, these traits will become even more potent.

Care should be taken, for these people can become very dangerous if set to ill course. Temptation will be a companion to whatever they aspire to be, leading them to ruin if they lack temperance.

The Manticore is either the best of man and lion or the worst of both. Those born under the Manticore, with a portion of the moon within the constellation, will have the worst temptations in correlation."

The temptation to use the worst words can correlate to many different things, dear readers. In the case of a world with powerful magicks, the implication of this is clear as crystal.

For those readers who would scoff at the idea that this is the definitive answer, you, of such scholarly mind as to understand that no record of very birth in the years that could be the time in question, clearly understand my problem.

This birth record is the best possible answer that is available to me, and if I cannot discount the possibility of her being a foreigner or merely a powerful witch that rose to power in another manner is beyond the scope of this search for truth.

Indulge me further, and you shall see how only one born from the city would be accepted by its rulers, and by its people. Only to the familiar do we accept the possibility of safety.

Part Three: From Child to Woman

It is not uncommon for the mundane of life to simply pass, just as water passes through an open hand. Within the archives of the academy, I found several examples of personal records from families that predate the current ruling elements.

The broad strokes of life for fifteen years placed down in merely a handful of pages. Most of these events are what you expect to quote, "It is a wonderous day as our child reaches their first year of life.

The child has begun speaking and walking just a short while ago, and it fills me with joy until I burst with tears." I do not see why the parents of this future despot would suspect anything.

While I am unable to find the personal journals of the patriarchs of the Geropalides or Archiplousios families, I have no sensible reason to suggest that any records kept from this time would indicate anything from standard course.

In my research I did discover that the effects of sorcery can manifest themselves in ways that would lead to shock and surprise.

In several statements of such incidents as recorded, "Our child became afflicted by something unseen. We saw the unexplained happen without reason.

The child suddenly erupted with power, bending the elements, made noises heard without apparent source, strange lights danced at their command, the powers of the profane or unearthly light would manifest, small things would defy nature by floating around."

These records give a glimpse into the sudden change for those afflicted by these "gifts".

Among the influential of the city, those who had the most tributes paid to them, or fidelity of families would have seen this as quite the problem with any of their children.

Being rumored to be different in such a way could influence the value of alliance or marriage.

Even in this age of greater freedom for the masses, marriage, for those but the poorest, is always an act of balance between the futures that could be and the station of the present.

In the past, well, things simply were not the same as they are today. The families that ran the city of Raven had a series of traditions and customs that locked them into the high places of the city.

Each family tried to measure its status amongst each other, along anything that numbers could be put to.

The amount of food grown on their land, the number of miners that paid them rents, their trade with our mountain neighbors, how much they could afford in lavish gifts, what they could build.

So many things that could line and divide and place neatly on the scale of one to twenty-four where a family sat. A young woman with such a talent may be forced to contain such powers, remain silent and hidden.

A rumor of such a curse could mean banishing your own child or sending them off far afield if you happened to know some mystic.

Citing these sources can point out the broad strokes of the year's unknown to all but those who lived them. Finally, I would like to remark on the environment these children would have grown in.

For such noble families, teaching their daughters to read and write would have been seen as practical.

However, deep academic study would have been seen as a final resort as compared to the arts, to the practical understanding of running a home, or interest in the way people converse.

So many things could have been happened left unwritten that I must leave up to your minds, dear reader, what could have been.

Whatever the despots' motivations during her rule, she was a person of flesh, blood, and soul as certainly as you are.

Part Four: Monsters of Shadow and Sand

"My name is Valen Lascaris, and this record is my recounting of the final moments of my old life.

The tribes of the deserts were always a potential threat, but their clan wars were always what prevented them from unifying under one banner. No one lord could ever control the numerous clans, families, or groups of raiders, bent on vengeance for the thefts and murders perpetuated on family after family.

The desert was always a cruel place, used as the executioner of the banished. Those made tough by the endless wandering normally approached the city cautiously, and normally with peaceful intent for trade.

I had thought we inspired awe and grandeur, that our mages and warriors would keep us safe from what might come. Though the militia and the soldiers fought well with shield and spear, our opponent's used bow and spear to their own great effect.

At their command seemed to be an order of desert mystics, capable of bring the raw earth to bear. They also trained birds to drop lit tinder into our city docks, leaving many ships burned and kept us from being able to fish easily.

Any cloth or canvas to keep the sun's burden light were destroyed. The worst of it was the surprise attacks at night, trying to mount the walls in the dead of night with no flame.

The invaders would dig to drain the ditches. They used their magic to damage the walls and even brought them down in a couple of places.

The message that came after that was simple. Those of low station within the walls would be allowed to live. The only heads they wanted were the current rulers, and if they got them, those who did so could expect a handsome reward.

Some surrendered willingly, begging to allow their children to live. Others fought in the streets and in their houses. I was knocked unconscious by the western gate by a mob trying to unlock the gate in their plan of salvation.

My men fought bravely and even held within a section of the tower but had to surrender the gate. That ended it. With two gates open we couldn't hold the streets. I could see the large homes in the square being overrun.

I did the only sensible thing at that point as our obligation was most likely being pulled from his quarters and slain. I offered for our men to lay down their arms if some leader would come by and accept our surrender.

Some seasoned veterans, dressed in well-crafted leather, with a dark complexion and ragged dark hair approached us.

Along his eyes I could see his age, and when he got close, some few silvery hairs sprouted from his shaggy, unkept beard.

His second spoke our tongue. "You have led men bravely and have fought with honor, turn over your weapon and be given peace. Your men shall be forgiven.

You all shall have a chance to join us." I had wished in that moment that I would have fought on, even though it would only serve vanity and destruction.

I did the harder thing and thought of my men, and the easier thing was to do what let them live. I handed over my spear, and my soldiers handed over their weapons as well.

The next couple of days went by simply enough. All of us who survived the siege were given water and food, and we were kept in tents outside the walls and away from armory stores.

Men would come by and give us wraps of cloth with some kind of symbol on them. Most likely claims of the family on the living relatives.

My men and I were claimed by one family. The symbol was a wyrm with arms but no wings and bearing no resemblance to the mighty winged beast.

I recall the day when I was brought before the child that would one day be prince of the city.

Six armed men came to the group of us and asked us to clean and prepare ourselves to meet our claimant.

We did as we instructed, so my group and I were walked through the still recovering city. Flies of all sorts were around, and we saw people going their way.

It seemed unreal to me. The enemies we had were all the things I feared but also saw in them the expression of civilized rule.

They were able to behead the rulers of our people, the base of our fidelity but extend to us opportunity to take our lives back. As we walked to the open market, this sense was simply magnified.

The square was full of the trade of human flesh, and the caring of those who would be brought in like their own sons and daughters. The price of being a ruler was on full display alongside the salvation of the low born.

The child sat in a fine chair, to either side of him were young men in merchants' robes and to either side of them veteran soldiers. The boy looked at me, far more disgusted than a child should be at that age.

He was unnaturally hard, and while his voice did not imbue him with supernatural strength, it was far crueler in tone than one expects. "Why are these soldiers here? They do not bear our sigil."

One of the merchants reached for a parchment note while the guards kept keen watch on us. Some words in the tongue were exchanged, the tone flat and calm.

The boy locked eyes on me. "You are a gift of manpower, given to my mother the queen of the Red Sands and now ruler of Kukori." He understood my tongue; it had finally registered.

The boy continues, "How did you survive the siege? You appear to be in better shape than the other citizens. Were you a warrior in the previous army?" He is perceptive, I thought.

He has a basic understanding, but I knew to choose my words well enough. "Yes, I was a guard captain in the Northwestern tower.

I led these militia in holding off any incursion along that section of wall and led a sally in trying to retake the western gate. It failed, and these few men are the survivors." He seemed unsatisfied with the truth.

"No!" He spoke with anger filling the edges of his words. "You are a surviving noble of some sort, hiding among these men. You were a leader, in charge." I knew in that moment I needed a believable lie.

Militia captains were not noble born; they were just trusted men of experience. I may be part of a desired vengeance from a group of raiders for all I knew.

I also thought it possible that he would have my men tortured to get his answer. Cruelty in such young eyes seems unbound. "My father was a member of the oligarchs, but my mother was a low born person," I began.

"He appointed me to the position when I reached age as an appeasement, and to relay information from a rival's household." The young boy sat in his chair, thinking over what had been said.

Oddly, I remember he tapped his right cheekbone as he thought as his last digits sat near his chin. He considered it deeply, and I kept my eyes locked on his. He finally sighed. "I suppose that you speak the truth.

You shall be sent to mother directly; your men shall be kept for labor within my family's house." His attention turned beyond my eyes and to my men as a group.

"You all shall take up your old skills and serve as builders of our house within the city. You shall be able to pursue your works without the worry of being called to war again.

Our people will protect you from outsiders." The line felt well-worn in speech, probably well-rehearsed and uttered several times a day.

The walk to the manor houses of the district was a rare occurrence for me. Only if requested was I made to walk a ruler back to their home. Perhaps an unruly youth needed returning.

Those kinds of things were the only reason that I would find myself on these paved streets. Now, it was to meet with the new despot.

The house I was taken to used to belong to the Geropalides family; the fine home was beset by flies. "Flies feast on the blood and flesh of us all" was my morbid reaction.

While the viscera had most likely been well washed, a few spots always seem to draw the creature's attention.

I was walked into the meeting chamber; these chambers dominate the center of the house and are used to receive the guest by the patron.

She sat in a beautifully crafted chair of a reddish wood; a barely visible pillow of worn velvet peeked from under her in a rare purple hew.

The robes were earthen tones and wraps of layers of cloth covered her body. Her dark hair caressed her cheek under her hood. A transparent cloth covered her face gently, and her eyes were enchanting dark pools of blue.

She lifted her chin to speak, and the words were charming. "Please approach and let us be as friends to one another." I felt her words ride through me, and I knew she could be trusted with her power.

"What has brought you to me, servant of the Sandworm Clan?" Her question felt so genuine, almost like she wanted to know what I thought of it all.

"I have been sent to be a servant to you," I started. "I fought along the western wall during the siege. My men and I surrendered after some citizens threw open the gate and we failed to close it in time."

She looked at me and listened the entire time, measuring my words and emotions. I felt myself so drawn to this beautiful ruler, unable to think how she could so rapidly become a friend to me in this situation.

She was merciful and caring, not anything like I could expect given the harsh and cruel fighting I had gone through the past few weeks. She let me talk, asking a few questions about me.

"Who are your parents? Do you have any surviving family? Would you tell me of your men and commanders?" It went on for a few hours, the most delightful conversation about everything in my life.

I was struck at that time with a strong realization: My mind had been clouded to her designs. It was too late in that moment.

She smiled. "Thank you for everything. All of this will be very helpful to ensuring that what must be done shall be." She continued, her words and beauty becoming more intimidating.

My mind felt bound, terrorized, and unable to escape her. "I will need the help of some experienced men to serve as my urban companions.

Making sure that fires do not ruin the docks, that people are inside in the night hours, that the stores of water and food are not harmed." She walked closer, tracing her finger down my cheek to my throat.

"Someone with experience in leadership, that the old guard would recognize should serve as captain. Someone the people of this city can trust with their safety." Menace dripped in her next sentence.

"Someone who has family that needs him to protect them. A young sister perhaps. Such rough men taking what trophies they felt earned from among the old rulers."

Her voice trailed off as she walked off, her hand drifting away. "Kneel, swear your fealty to me on your sister's life, and I will make you a captain within the urban companions."

She didn't need to say what the other option was. Manipulated and threatened, but with no other recourse I swore my oath. In time I would come to realize that she understood the road she walked was filled with death.

I guess looking back on those days, when I think of the queen, she just wanted to know where the assassins were coming from.

Part Five: The Witch-Queen's Rule

For the length of the Queen Adoniah's rule, the populace would know both safety and fear. The days following the conquest of Kukori saw the death of anyone who was capable of a legitimate claim to power. Anyone who had run any affairs of note were taken to the town square and had their heads removed.

Along the walls these grizzly trophies served as clear warnings that our new rulers wanted obedience and order. The people of Kukori became familiar with the clans of the Red Sands, the wandering tribes of the waste. Nine such clans had made claim to the bounty and wealth taken by the old oligarchs.

The ones that mattered it seemed were the clans of Sandwyrm, Black Eagle, and Wild Dog. The banners of all the clans now stood on poles or were hung from the walls of homes and guard posts. What matters is that each clan head was bound to the queen, and she decided how spoils were ultimately shared.

My job was simple enough, lead a small coalition of these peoples around the city as a watch. From what I can tell, the clan heads handled internal matters. When interclan violence or crime happened, clan heads figured out what had to happen in the city. Grievances would be handled in a few straightforward ways.

If rightfully owned property was stolen, the thief returned it with another half of value or faced death by their own clan. Violence on fellow clanmates was only permitted to solve personal issues, and in equal measure to an offense.

Death was brought about either swiftly or through the act of banishment to the waste. Over the next few years, things remained calm. The common folk simply kept their focus on the turning of one season unto the next.

The clan rulers finished carving their appropriate portions of the city, which they ruled in the name of the queen and the prince. The open trade that came from across the northern shores, and the interactions with the other cities across the desert and on the eastern shores were missions of peace and trade.

My task did not put me in the rooms when these talks took place; however, I met many of these foreign dignitaries for a few minutes. Escorting them from ship through the city, I was asked several questions. Every diplomat wanted to know about the queen, about the clans, about how the mining was going.

The most interesting time came four years after the initial capture of the city and the arrival of a dwarven diplomat, our mountain allies. I had never seen them come to us and had only heard tales of their stout and strong frames.

I presume the diplomat was of midlife when I met him. His face was weathered and wrinkled, indicating a tougher life than I would think a diplomat would live. He did not share any words with me, but I could tell he was resolved to his business.

His beard sat on his chest, well ordained, and scented with some kind of rare herb. His armor was of stout iron, a rare sight. He wore a tabard that indicated the royal house of our allies, and he was most likely a relative for such a mission.

The diplomatic mission turned out to be the arrival of a regiment of strong soldiers from the mountains. My responsibility in that time was to keep clansmen and dwarf from coming to violence inside the city. There were a few incidents in the bars and streets, nothing unexpected.

The call eventually came throughout the city. The queen sent her soldiers to join the regiment of dwarves to assault the Spearbreaker tribe within the canyons of the Red Sands. A request for volunteers from the city and offer of reward was given for those of the old militia to join.

My surviving brothers were torn, but the allure of a better life called, and they could not leave it unanswered. So, they marched to the desert, and I was left with nothing but prayers and uncertainty of what would become of this force.

Part Six: Fifty Days

Within the journal of Captain Valen Lascaris I found, dear readers, a copy of the official report of a battle that took place at The Weeping Oasis.

This seems to have been an encounter with a well-coached group of monstrous beings that roam the desert, with some malefactor heading this vile coalition.

Queen Adoniah led a force that seems to be roughly between nine hundred to twelve hundred individuals. The official report is cited to one nobleman who served with the queen at the time of the incident.

Obviously, I could not get any other source as the opposing force was killed and were probably not fond of recording anything of value anyway. It reads thus:

"I am Arzani, third son of Arsha, scion of clan head Mozik who by rights of conclave rules the clan.

Over the course of fifty days a collection of warriors of the nine clans, their slaves, and nearly three hundred mercenaries from the Dwarven Enclave gathered to assault the Weeping Oasis.

Our march lasted nearly a week, as the long days of Solys keep the hours of desert marching short. The army was able to survive on its carried rations made in the city beforehand.

These sands offer very little in the way of food, unless you have developed a taste for well-cooked insects or small amounts of meat of snakes and foxes. Water is a far more precious commodity anyway.

The few druids with us along with the clerics of Anarus, the most holy lord of the sun, kept us from dying of thirst. The march was otherwise left unchallenged as it went along in moonlight.

In the early morning of Moonsday, we spotted several obstacles that broke up the hills overlooking The Weeping Oasis.

Scouting found several families of ogre's and their slaves polluting the water with their presence. The Spearbreaker clan had plenty of help, and some kind of devious leader to prepare the battleground.

It took two weeks of skirmishes and a few hundred losses to push these beasts beyond most of their defensive works before we could force a pitched battle.

The dwarven mercenaries held the center, creating the strongest chevron in the center. The right chevron shield wall consisted of the militia with supporting pike.

The left was comprised of our noble retainers and ourselves and supporting wing of the queen's Horseguard. We withstood a shock of enemy missile and returned in kind before engaging with spear and axe.

The horsemen waited while the dwarves slowly fell back under the assault. Once the enemy was in the thralls of bloodlust, the horsemen were signaled and hammered our foes.

It was a simple matter of killing those who had lost sense of the changing tide. The Spearbreaker patriarch was split on no less than three lances, and his arms and legs hung from posts to warn the other ogres.

The survivors rested and took the dead to be given rights and burned, and the holy men set to mending the oasis. After collecting anything of value, we reassembled and marched home.

Some of the camp followers were searched along the way.

It seems that a few among them are quite crafty, but we decided that if no one was truly left without some reward, then their price for service was left be.

I do recall yelling at one of them in the distance. They seemed overly keen at going over the left arm of the Spearbreaker Patriarch. Once she saw we had spotted them, they quickly disappeared from view.

That is all of note for the five weeks absent of the city." It is here, my reader that I found something most peculiar. In transcribing this passage, some portions of the page seemed elevated.

While difficult to notice at first, I discovered this page was more dense than other parchment folded within. Some solvent was able to lift the copy of this record and show a personal passage hidden beneath. Captain Valen Lascaris's words continue from his journal here.

I plan on covering these words under another page, for they could be the death of me. I feel that I should keep record of the truth that transpired within, should the queen herself choose to act. I will, of course, prepare a false report to ensure that the prince will not report whatever misfortune befell me in his mother's absence.

I had never been so fearful of the fall of light. Fifty days under the prince, now nearly a man, would prove to be the most undesirable of my time. I write these passages understanding that if they are found, they will never be known to the world. My nights are filled with terrible screams and sinister laughter.

The prince has taken to a new hobby with a few of his soldiers. He has been playing magister, allowing his companions all sorts of liberties.

The terrorize the populace that we may not rise from our low born position. One night they tore five people from a small home. They dragged them into the street, screaming of conspiracy to murder the prince.

Notes they had so conveniently found on the subject were thrown in their faces. The father in the family was beaten with a variety of implements from a local smithy shop. He wouldn't confess at first, trying to proclaim his innocence only to have teeth broken along with the bones in his feet.

When they grabbed his youngest boy, he screamed his guilt. I wish it had helped, but the malevolence of those boys. They were far more monster than anything I could have encountered. The prince did not just kill this man, which should have been enough.

He ordered the man tied to a roughhewn post in the square, then demanded his family gather in front of him. People were summoned from their homes, and my guard was forced to keep the peace. His sons were butchered, and their entrails thrown to the dogs.

His wife was surrounded and stoned to death by his guards. The prince grabbed the man's eldest daughter and pronounced her service as a personal slave as compensation for his crime. After forcing the man to see his entire family, all the things a man could love to be destroyed, the prince gave his companions permission to end him.

They tortured him for hours longer, tearing at him like starving jackals. Hot tongs tore flesh from him, and they spent time hacking apart his body. The misery inflicted on him for everyone to see made the hope die in my chest. Nine more such incidents took place, all in similar fashion.

All the girls and women the prince and his cohorts took were either never seen again or found in one of the places with the working girls left scarred from flesh to soul. I tried to pray, but when I did, I just saw faces locked in misery and horror.

I cannot sleep; the faces and the screams haunt me in everything I do. I would have thought battle to prepare me better, but in battle a warrior has hope and control. These people were just slaughtered for fun in the guise of justice and order, and my men and I had to watch.

A messenger from the army arrived in the night forty-nine days after the army had left. The late evening saw the remains of the army led by our queen. It resembled a crippled man, hobbling with a staff, painfully making every step.

It the moonlight, the queen and her retinue of veterans strode their horses as if leading a grand army. The southern gates of the city opened, and she proceeded to the plaza square.

Her bodyguard flanked the returning warriors, and I did my best to count the dead. Twelve hundred men of all kinds left the city in proud formation.

Nearly a third of them had not returned, and nearly a quarter carried some type of injury. The militia, my friends who had left seeking a better life, were all but annihilated.

I tried to remember the words the queen spoke before disbanding them. "Before I can release you fine and noble warriors with your new-found wealth and glory, I beg of you a short time for proper words. I extend my gratitude to our allies, who came from their great hall and brought death to our enemies.

I extend my deepest love from my subjects, great and small, who would see our futures made bright. The Spearbreaker clan and all its allies lay defeated. Our desert routes to trade and the great oasis belong to us. We have truly mastered our home. Kukori welcomes you back into her warm bosom, that you may feel the cool breeze upon your faces. Your queen declares your obligations fulfilled, go in honor and dignity." She turns her steed, and she and her bodyguards ride from the square.

The prince and his jackals follow suit, and the army is no more.

Most of the survivors find their way into drinking, others limp and stumble along the paving stones to their homes. I hear it all as I walk the streets, joyful sobs, and angry curses.

I had a chance to speak with one of the lone survivors from the militia, one of maybe fourth or so of the nearly five hundred volunteers. What Peleus told me drove the sorry of the last few weeks back into my heart.

"The march across the Red Sands was easy," Peleus began. "The army marched in the cool night and early dawn hours. It took us the first week to gather near the oasis claimed by the Spearbreaker clan.

Those damn ogres, they got their wits somehow. They had moved stones into half circle breaks, made it, so we couldn't fight 'em straight on. Every one of those piles of rock had to be taken.

It took us and our dwarven mercs 'round fifteen days to kill off all the ogres 'nd such holdin' these spots. The whole time, being harassed by something with magic." I stopped them.

"Did you say one of these monsters had true magic?" Peleus nodded to confirm his words.

"By this time water had been rationed for at least five days and we could start to smell the oasis even on still air.

Her majesty could see that starved look in our eyes, which is when she ordered the rest of us in. We had the dwarves and horsemen at our backs and on the wings, and we fought with everything we had left.

As we fell, our overlords pushed us on. We walked right over the corpses of friend and foe alike. We thought they would break, try and run. They fought us till the last." Peleus hung in that moment, taking a deep breath.

Exhaling he continued, "The queen finally pushed her bodyguard into it, letting them crash along the enemy left. That finally scattered any enemy not deep in bloodlust." Peleus paused, a moment of thought on his brow.

I asked, "What else did you see?" I was trying to assure him that he could unburden himself, that his was for me.

"S-something was really wrong with the ogre chieftain. His skin was deep blue and black. His hands had great claws on the end of them, and even though he was dead, I was still very afraid." I feel like Peleus saw something more than he was letting me know. No such ogre matching that look had even been seen by anyone I knew. That in and of itself was not what worried Peleus.

I stopped them. "I can tell something else really frightened you, but I will let it go. It is better I am left unaware?"

Peleus looked at me square. "Best not to talk about it." He noted that the dead were burned, and that the wounded were given care, and after a few days of collecting goods from the fallen and refilling our water that the army, damaged, we left.

I remember taking a walk to the shrine of Cyhaldir, the shining guardsman. Cyhaldir is our god of soldiers, exemplified for his order and his bravery for any mission.

It is said that he watches over those who fight for their commanders with loyalty and courage. I found myself unable to beg for his aid anymore. I pulled his symbol from underweight my armor.

The simple wooden token, a round shield with a crossing mace and axe, and tossed in onto the feet of the statue. I turned my back and headed to my house. In that moment, the city could fall into the sea, and I would welcome it.

Part Seven: One Deadly Dance

The last entry of Captain Valen Lascaris, leader of the night watch company of the urban companions.

Tonight, is the coronation of Prince Eshmun, eldest son of Queen Adoniah. It is a night that I have feared for the last seven years. That this monster that wears the skin of a man would survive every one of his sick acts to become King.

The prince's degenerate and perverse taste have made my job as Captain of the Night Companions an ever-mounting list of problems. He and his jackals pick apart anyone they feel like as the mood strikes them.

I know in my heart of few of his victims were plotting a vengeance against him. I can only imagine what the few survivors would be consumed with grief and a desire for vengeance.

Just this season, two separate individuals tried to shoot him as he rode through the city. His armor proved strong enough, and their aim poor enough.

After every such attempt on the life of a clan head, or the prince, the horrors were elevated beyond their standard. Queen Adoniah, for her part, seemed to be able to find any criminal through her powers.

Prince Eshmun would simply send the royal guardsman to round up the family in question and publicly torture everyone until he was bored or felt that no more messages could be taken in by the onlookers.

It certainly kept the attempts low, and everyone became excepting of this monster living among them. Merchants from all places started to sense the fear and travelers did not want to stay.

The stories of the despair of the lowest and those who angered the rulers made it along the winds of ships or beyond the farmlands. The dwarves of North Highland even went so far to bar visits from the prince or any diplomat directly.

As he is now approaching twenty, the regency of Queen Adoniah is now coming to an end. As much as the queen did not interact with her subjects, she also tended to let them live unharmed if they showed obedience.

I never got to see her in court, but I did read the ordinances passed from various rulings. The queen had a greater understanding of how to use justice and understood how to cross the line into cruelty just enough.

She ruled as King Arkouda had, a firm hand that could exact a strong toll. The queen let her son have more power, and it simply revealed a more and more sinister madman. So, I have had enough of it all.

Every scream echoed in the dark shadows of my mind, and every bit of bloody business for the last eight years must come to a close. I cannot say that what I am doing is going to be within the bounds of the written law.

I have a plan on this night of grand coronation, and that is to ensure that the lesser of two evils remains in power. The plans for this long night feast have had to be given to me as normal course of security.

The festivities will include several contests of arms, plenty of drinking and carousing, and a grand display of dancing. Dozens of slave women will be forced to dance for several hours and serve as companions for all involved.

I have made sure that some of these entertainers are some of the former victims of the prince. If one of them is unable to get to him, then I plan to place a poisoned blade directly into his black heart.

I must admit I feel very foolish writing nearly everything in my journal, but I have made arrangements for this record to be recovered from its hiding place this evening.

My sister, brother-in-law and their children have already been spirited away via cargo ship. The price to the thief's guild was steep, but I will not be alive to suffer the consequences of this action if I succeed.

I have made sure to have a fast-acting poison to swallow should this plot fail. Should this record somehow fall into the hands of my enemies, well, I am sorry to any of my subordinates who suffer in my place.

I am left to only speculate on how the end happened, but certainly I can say that the records have nothing of this prince's decrees or ordinances.

His signature is unable to be found on any declaration or treaty, so I am forced to conclude that the plot achieved its aim. I want to warn the reader to caution the idea of the dear Captain succeeding on his own.

Many people were all aware of this assassination attempt, and any one of them could have warned another authority figure. My best working theory is that one or more of the clan heads backed this play.

With the only known heir of Queen Adoniah dead, this would leave the more powerful clans to perhaps name their own successor in the event of her death.

The clan heads could have also been trying to increase their own power as her major influencing council. At the very least it is also possible one of the clans had a vendetta on the man given his dark and dangerous habits.

Part Eight: Whispers of Hope

Ledger entries from "Black Cobra", a codename for which I cannot find the true owner.

"It's been only a few months since the news hit the town that the prince died at his big party. He got his own nice stone box just inside Zuzara's temple, at least it was nice when they built it.

Every man, woman, and child that dares have pissed on that grave. I must admit though, nothing brings people together like a bastard everyone wants dead. Business though, it has been a bit harder sense his death.

The new guy in charge of night patrols is a real hard ass, trying to impress her majesty or some such trash. My crew came in tonight with a few interesting tidbits, and some success.

My working girl "White Lilac" got us some information on the upcoming big trade ship from down south. Apparently, they are bringing some rare gems as gifts for the clan heads, and if we can get aboard, we can turn a nice profit.

"Silverstring" spent most of the day playing his music and just cut us in on a third of his hat money. Not too bad of a take, and he even got himself an in with a servant for Clan Wild Dog.

If he can charm his way inside, he might be able to liberate a few pieces for our collection. "Greenmask" is our newest crew member, and they are certainly high-end potential.

Great confidence and seems to slip in and out places and personalities like a good thief goes in and out of second story windows. They are probably moonlighting or doing some solo work on the side, and I almost care.

If they pull the wagon, and I get my cut of profits. Greenmask gave me a heads up on overhearing some slaves trying to put together a collection of stuff to trade for weapons.

It's got me worried; I've only heard of that stuff ending badly. The queen has some way of findin' this kinda stuff out and putting it out very quickly and with a hard boot stomp."

Ledger entries associated with "White Lilac":

"If respectable work paid more than starving, I may not have resorted to this line of work. I think about what happened to my sister and I though, and I guess I am just making good of this horrible situation.

Last year the prince and his lackies decided they need new entertainers for the month, and she and I happened to be fancied by some shit for brains in the prince's service.

I never saw my sister after that and wound up on my ass and homeless forty days later. I hope whoever killed the prince cut off his manhood first. Well, work tonight was worth it.

A very jolly sailor with a desire for company was kind enough to let me know about the Sea Otter trade ship and its very rich cargo. Apparently, some gifts are coming for the clan heads.

I wonder what the other city states are up to? I do not know if they truly think they can bribe their way into the best deals, but they will have to do it on a smaller budget.

I certainly hope that I can get a fresh start somewhere far from here. I could say that my husband died at sea, and I am a widow looking for a new life. Maybe I could convince someone that I am a runaway from a loveless marriage.

I just know that I won't carry on like this anymore. "Black Cobra" is cold hearted and dangerous, and I work *very* hard to not be on the end of his fatal bite. I remember him finding a customer who thought he did not have to pay.

He took a hammer to five of his fingerbones and said that if he ever tried it again, he would bury that hammer in his head. Word got around quick in the docks to pay me first and to leave me in the condition I was found in.

I worked with "Silverstring" in the nicer taverns from time to time, getting jobs and lifting some coins from pockets. I'd marry him, but I know where he's been. Silverstring can always make me laugh though, so that's good.

Greenmask is a very interesting character. She, he, or they, I can hardly tell with all the changes of disguise. Every time is very lifelike and even the voices change so believable. It must be magic.

When they talk to me about what they hear, it feels hopeful—a little too hopeful. With the queen's child dead, it seems everyone in the city is starting to find courage and small acts of defiance.

Nobody has completely lost their minds and done anything directly to the queen, but I get the sense that people are starting to cross into that territory. I would rather not be here if and when that happens."

Ledger entries associated with "Silverstring":

"Oh, only to have the blessing of the muse of the pen when I keep my journal. This is a rather tedious piece of work, and my words better spent on rhyme and melody.

Black Cobra insists I engage in this activity. He seems convinced that these notations will be of some use later. He said it would help me retain details, but I have never needed such a tool.

He seems to have forgotten that I had to memorize no less than a dozen songs and two dozen different poems just to meet some basic expectations of my instructors.

Head mistress Khole was very willing to help me, into the early morning, if memory serves. Ah, she was very skilled in all her instructions. However, words could not give such things due justice.

In main function of this journal, tonight activities included musical performance for coin and some carousing in order to help my good friend White Lilac into the good pockets of the sailors from far afield.

While she was working information from some of them, I listened to their yards. I also made sure to pass along about the unfortunate passing of the prince, to ensure that good news travels the world.

Among the docks and streets, those who have only their lives to lose are the first to cheer and mock the slain.

For my part it's hard not to imagine what type of humorous and insulting poems I could make, but I like my tongue in my head. I think Black Cobra has some kind of score to settle within the circle of the queen.

I get that feeling with the more dangerous missions he is willing to gather all of us for. The stress of these life-threatening missions is starting to get to me, and I find myself trying to do anything to steel myself.

Black Cobra wants to make a real hit by stealing from a trade family that is trying to impress the city. All those treasures could set us all for life, and I cannot imagine that this will not be the biggest test to date.

Part Nine: The Head of a Monster

Records recovered from the cases of Thoas Gelonidis, Amathea Irinias, and Brison Kyrilakos as tried before the Royal Tribunal of Queen Adoniah. Chief Magister Doruk of the Sandwyrm clan leads the investigation.

Court would have most likely been held within the walls of the palace. Which room I cannot be certain. However, the descriptions seem to indicate a smaller room with a window to let it midday and evening light.

"The charges of treason and conspiracy to criminal acts against the peoples of Kukori is called before the freeman Thoas Gelonidis, who stands accused by her majesty Queen Adoniah rightful ruler of this city and its surroundings.

How does the defendant plead?"

"Innocent", replies Thoas. "We have been informed by no less than six individuals that you were not hired by any officer of the ship. You were caught carrying a very expensive item off board.

When confronted by the ship's guards, you ran. An urban companion caught you shortly thereafter with several gemstones that were in your possession. Gems that were in the manifest and missing from aboard the Sea Otter."

"I have an explanation for all of this, your lordship," Thoas stated.

Doruk sighs. "Proceed, Thoas. I would like to know how all of this came to pass."

Thoas begins, "I was simply running a night errant. I had been contracted by a prominent lady to collect her gifts promptly. She simply would not wait until the morning, so as a known porter, I decided to ask myself aboard and go about my business."

"Who is this noble woman who employed you?" asked Doruk.

"Your mother," replies Thoas. Chief Magister Doruk has Thoas removed from the chamber and sent below for interrogation.

"The charges of treason and conspiring to criminal acts against the peoples of Kukori is called before Amathea Irinias, standing accused by her majesty Queen Adoniah rightful ruler of the city and its surroundings.

How does the defendant plead?"

"Innocent," replies Amathea.

"You were brought in by urban companions while in the vicinity of the Sea Otter while it was being stolen from. The records indicate that you were discovered alongside two men *ahem* in a state of undress. These men were on guard for the Sea Otter, and they were being distracted by you."

Amathea responds, "There is no reason to think I had any idea what was happening outside on the docks. I was earning a wage, and that activity has nothing to do with those charges."

Doruk inquires, "Who do you work for?"

"Whoever pays me for my company, lordship," replies Amathea.

"Who do you pay for protection?" Doruk asks.

"I pay the Black Cobras on the waterfront when I work there," Amathea replies.

Doruk produces a drawing of Thoas, and inquires, "Do you recognize this man?"

Amathea appears to look and dismiss the image, "The Black Cobras wear masks when they take coin, so I can't be sure."

Magister Doruk appears satisfied and produces one more picture, "Can you tell me who this is?" The picture is of a young woman, similar in appearance to Amathea, such as a family member. "Do you recognize the woman in this drawing?"

"Yes," says Amathea, the reply less audible than her earlier testimony.

"Please identify her for our records," Doruk sternly demands.

Amathea again answers in a more matter-of-fact tone, "Niobe Irinias, my sister." Doruk then places the following before Amathea.

"You were conscripted for use in a conspiracy against the rightful ruler of the city, to steal from her loyal subjects and commit those riches against her in a plot of revenge for your dead sister. Do you deny this? If you do, then you may repeat your testimony within the circle of truth, and we can dismiss you." Amathea simply remained silent for the remainder of the inquiry.

Doruk concludes, "Her majesty shall have the truth, from either you or your employer and by force if it must be that way." Amathea is removed from the chamber.

"The charges of treason and conspiracy to criminal acts against the peoples of Kukori is called before freeman Brison Kyrilakos, who stands accused by her majesty Queen Adoniah rightful ruler of this city and its surroundings. How does the defendant plead?"

"Guilty of it all," replies Brison. "However, I will not beg for mercy under any circumstances," Brison adds. The magisters exchanged a look and Doruk responds to Brison.

"If you do not deny the charges then the court sentence you to death by drawing and quartering. Your sentence will be carried out at weeks end. You can only receive the mercy of a swift axe if you tell us who else joined you."

Brison appears to consider the offer for a moment but answers, "No, I cannot give up my compatriots in this. I mean, it's so many people clandestinely ending this royal house. I couldn't possibly even name them all."

The tribunal appears agitated. "Who are you working with? We want your conspirators!" Doruk is unsettled in this moment.

Brison begins, "Like I said I couldn't tell you all the names even if I wanted to. Everyone, your superiors included, are concerned with the queen letting her son get killed like that. It shows a weakness, an inability to protect her own family, or even a willingness to let her own kid die for power. The question you should be asking is how we got caught."

Magister Doruk responds flatly, "Your groups hubris finally caught up with all of you. That is why the three of you are before me; your plans have fallen apart."

Brison responds, "That is entirely possible, but it seems odd that this well worked plan on lesser ships seems to work just fine. No, I think you had help. Mystic arts investigating on your behalf. Now you need to wonder, if we thought you would catch us, why would we go forward with it in the first place. Also, you should know we have a four-crew member that you don't have in custody."

Doruk looks at Brison intensely, seething under clenched jaw. "What do you think you have accomplished? You are grandstanding without a point. You and your allies are currently in our jail cells, and you have no end goal."

Brison smiles in his reply, "Actually our end goal has either been achieved or is in the midst of completion. Chief magister, you won't get any further information from the rest of us."

After looking at these records, I have concluded this was the tip of the spear. Thirty cases of theft and assault on the clan head homes took place over the course of just two nights, a massed assault by the gangs.

It appears that the palace grounds were infiltrated, but any records of what happened there are long destroyed. I am left to only a single conclusion; it appears that the thief cabals figured out where the diviners were.

It would not be unreasonable for the queen to employ several mystics capable of scrying on high value targets in order to maintain their safety. She could also use them to spy on her subjects and search out treason.

If these people were killed or captured, then this would blind the queen to any designs on replacing her. With the death of her son, the clan heads may have seen this as making her unfit to rule.

Perhaps the laws before her simply meant that when he died, it was another man's position to rise to. Without full records of the tribes, I can only speculate. These events lead to the last days of Queen Adoniah's rule.

Part Ten: Long Knives, Longer Shadows

Recovered from the record of Lykoreias, survivor of the overthrow of Queen Adoniah.

"While I lay here a few days and nights removed from these events, I cannot understand how or why I was allowed to live. That day started with a tension, a feeling like a fire was going to erupt under our feet.

The morning hours were a buzz of wandering patrols, and business for the main square. The day was set for several executions at the sun's apex, and the preparations for the condemned were completed.

Conspirators and criminals, the normal if all too common set of crimes. I had seen several of these types of executions, but even I had my reservations.

My commander felt the same. "Something isn't going the way we have it planned," he had remarked quietly. The magister and executioners arrived in their timely way, preparing for their given duties.

The executioners prepared the wheel and their clubs and blades. The magister stood at forward of the area of execution and gave a command to open the street.

Five men and two women, all chained about the neck, hands, and feet, were marched through the crowd. This act used to cause the people of the city to erupt in anger.

Normally they would spit or jeer; they might rain shit and piss and rotten food upon their heads. The silence from the crowd caused a lump in my throat, I forced it down and tried to focus.

The quiet murmurs of the onlooks fell when the magister read out the charges of the condemned. "Before the people of Kukori, these men and women are brought for sentencing for the crimes of larceny, conspiracy, and treason.

Thoas Gelonidis, Amathea Irinias, Brison Kyrilakos, Simmias, Marcian, Fyrruda, and Koragos all stand united in a conspiracy to steal from our great nobles and use these goods and money to arm a rebellion against the queen.

They have confessed to all of these crimes, and as such, in the name of Anarus our mighty lord of sun, we place the righteous judgement before these people who would see rightful rule undone and give us anarchy."

While the magister spoke, I had noticed some slight movement in the crowd as well as the early arrival of some carrion birds sitting and waiting.

Somewhere from the crowd, a cloaked figure tossed a large sack that landed with a wet thud. The magister looked disgusted at the bag, and while no one could find the figure, he began to search the mysterious container.

Within peeked out the head of some blue green ogre, its eyes open and seeming very much alive. In that moment of horror, the executioner and magister were rushed by several figures in the crowd carrying a variety of tools.

Before the small contingent of guard could react, the crowd had turned to free the traitors. The commander swiftly called for our retreat as we engaged and pushed back towards the palace, keeping the crowd from advancing.

Battles broke out all over the city as the clan heads tried to save themselves from the groundswell. The city being mostly stone meant that the fires were less dangerous, except at the docks.

The first few hours were of the palace guard, and those still loyal fighting to secure routes to our other points of resistance within the city.

All of the cities lowest seemed to have come together and ambushed anyone who travelled about the streets. From the palace walls I saw some of the clans even doing battle with one another.

The fighting skirmishes and ambushes, no one stood in pitched battle. The everyday fish and butchering knives became the most violent of blades.

Those who could get hold of anything heavy would beat anyone in heavy armor to death by simply overwhelming him with numbers and beating them to death and stabbing through any openings in the plates or in the rings of mail.

As the sun settled over the horizon, those of us still in the palace were forced to attempt a breakout to the west gate and escape to the mountains. Fighting in the twilight and the torchlight became ever more desperate.

All of the men and I were breathing heavy and sweating; the day had done in our resolve and endurance. We were being picked off from inside the windows of building, or from their roofs.

Tiro, a swordsman to my right, was killed with a jagged tile hurled with great force. It cut out his eye and crushed his face.

In the night, we ran into a dense mob and the melee became a frenzy against the tidal wave of violence. They broke after a few dozen of them were cut down, but I received a grievous wound and laid against a wall.

Blood. Blood ran down the streets, between the cracks of the paving stones. It looked more like dirty water or ink as it ran its course, but the smell could not be hidden from my mind.

The blood slowly streamed from me, mingling with earth and stone. The blood slid down to comingle with that of fallen foes and friends alike. Fire made shadows dance along the street and up and down the walls of stone.

Distance shouts and screams pierced the night along with an undertone of pained miserable whimpers from the dying around me.

The sounds of several warriors and the clap hooves of a single horse started winding their way closer and closer, but unsure in that moment of the danger, I remained still and quiet.

Soldiers dressed in the armor and shadow black cloaks of the royal guard along with a woman on horseback eventually came into view.

The royal guard were dressed for menace and fear, with blackened bronze that covered them nearly in entirety, their helms, and neck guards, blinded them to their sides.

This encouraged an unwavering stare that looked only forward. The person I had saw upon the horse I had not recognized in the moment but knew them to be important.

Only when the light from errant flame danced, did I begin to recognize the face of my queen. As quickly as I recognized it, it shifted away, and a green cloth covered the eyes under a cloak of a stranger.

"He's still alive. Tend to him." One of the soldiers removed his helmet, revealing the face of Thoas Gelonidis, who said, "Are you sure? I mean, he was trying to kill us earlier."

The person laughed. "If we killed people for that, there would be four people left in the city."

Thoas shook his head. "Suppose that's true. Alright, boy, hold this bandage against you and don't die."

After that, I woke up the next day with water and bandages with some of the city's residents going about trying to clean up. The clan heads were either dead or had somehow managed to escape the city over that night.

The next couple of days, I imagine the gang leaders started to figure out they were in charge and how to come to what agreements.

I never learned of what happened of Queen Adoniah, but without her corpse, I imagine she somehow escaped in the madness. A few people say her strongest guards procured a trade vessel, and they fled to the west.

Once I am healed, I am heading out to a quiet life of farming and leaving all of this behind me, and I will count myself grateful to be alive."

Epilogue: Another story, perhaps?

The young merchant looked over the short tome, hiding whatever feeling he had from Myron. The old man had spent some sixty days acquiring all of his research and having copied it into his book.

With a simple star and crescent of the moon for a cover, bound in beautiful blue dyed leather. The glittery gold trim of the illuminated text showed a well-crafted piece. He closed the man's work and carefully looked at him.

"Are you sure this was everything you could find? I had thought that a Queen of Raven would have had a grander legacy." The young man flipped his braided hair from his shoulder and looked with intent on the man's answer.

"It is true that much of the record was lost, and I imagine that the forebears of Clan Nevar wanted to erase any chance that someone would resurrect any old claims." The old man was well assured in his investigation.

Myron continued, "It could also be that some of the crimes of Queen Adoniah were also perpetrated by some of those who would eventually become part of the clan system in Raven today.

Obviously, they wouldn't show anyone such black marks and would try to erase such things if they could." The young merchant held his chin in his hand for a moment, contemplating other questions.

"What did the ogre head have to do with anything?" This was a detail that perhaps needed more context. The old man mused, stroking his graying stubble before answering.

"I have no good knowledge of how magic works. However, the dark attributes given Queen Adoniah may indicate she was able to draw a certain kind of power from it. Also, it seems she kept a few mystics with diving powers.

Those people could have formed the base of her spy network, used to keep her clan heads and enemies in line."

The merchant nodded in approval. "Thank you, and of course here is your payment."

The merchant hands over a small leather bag containing a few precious stones worth nearly three hundred golden coins.

The old man is very pleased and with a great smile says, "Your lordship, it was a pleasure working on this for you. If you need of me again, please send someone to find me. You are a most generous patron."

The young lord dismisses him with a hand, and the old man moves away in proper custom and goes about his afternoon.

From another room in the house a woman nearly forty with blond-gray hair and light-colored eyes enters. She walks with a confidence and purpose, approaching the young noble as he turns.

He smiles, and she returns it. "I did as you asked, here is everything that could be garnered on the subject in question." The merchant smiles holding the book up in his left hand, and she places her hand upon it.

"What about the researcher?"

Her words linger with a dark anticipation before he replies, "Assassins will end his life and take his gems as payment."

They continue with locked eyes, with the merchant saying, "I know that I will receive my gift before you receive your book." His demands were easily understood in the moment. She simply smiles.

She speaks a few words he cannot understand, and then she kisses him deeply, causing him to release the book. They embrace as the kiss continues, only for the merchant to begin to bleed and cough from his mouth.

In moments he is dead on the floor, and the blood along the front of the woman's clothes is black from some vile poison. She strides away from the merchant up into a corner of the building she had just come from.

In this moment, she thinks, "Sweet Kukori, it's been a long time. I have defied fate in returning to you, and you will be mine again." Her concentration shifts as the illusion slowly disappears.

As it dissipates, climbing up her legs revealing desiccated limbs wrapped in fine linens. Up her hips and torso, along her arms and finally passing her face. A female body, wrapped tightly in linens with dead flesh appearing in some places.

The eyes long gone, replaced with red gleaming pits of death and despair. She thinks, "You will be my city again, and every descendant of this rebellion will be my slave."

Don't miss out!

Visit the website below and you can sign up to receive emails whenever Triston Pethybridge publishes a new book. There's no charge and no obligation.

https://books2read.com/r/B-A-TFNV-ZTECC

BOOKS 2 READ

Connecting independent readers to independent writers.

Did you love *The Last Witch-Queen of Raven*? Then you should read *Blackbirds: Life of a Thief*[1] by Kyleen McHenry!

IMAGE COMING SOON[2]

Abandoned by his parents and taken in by Sean Willock, owner of the Gods Tavern in Stone Creek, Lonan was taught three things over the years: To steal, to fight, and to survive.

One day, it is revealed he is the son of The Morrigan, goddess of war and prophecy. Lonan stands on the edge of a never-ending battle between forces he does not understand. Will he embrace his destiny and start his path to becoming a true demi-god? Or will he turn his back and leave his home defenseless?

Read more at www.kyleenmchenry.com.

---

1. https://books2read.com/u/bwa0VO
2. https://books2read.com/u/bwa0VO

About the Publisher

Ky's Korner Productions, LLC is a media production company based in Berwick, Pennsylvania. They produce feature films, shorts, skits, television and web series, literature, and more. Check out their website for all their content.

www.kyskornerproductions.com

CPSIA information can be obtained
at www.ICGtesting.com
Printed in the USA
BVHW040945140523
663966BV00004B/5